AXEL WASHES THE RUG

Axel Washes the Rug

Story by *Tuula Pere*
Illustrations by *Nyamdorj Lkhaasuren*
Layout by *Peter Stone*
Edited by *Susan Korman*

ISBN 978-952-357-468-7 (Hardcover)
ISBN 978-952-357-469-4 (Softcover)
ISBN 978-952-357-470-0 (ePub)
First edition

Copyright © 2021 Wickwick Ltd

Published 2021 by Wickwick Ltd
Helsinki, Finland

Originally published in Finland by Wickwick Ltd in 2021
Axel Washes the Rug, ISBN 978-952-357-468-7

Axel Washes the Rug

TUULA PERE · NYAMDORJ LKHAASUREN

WickWick

Children's Books from the Heart

2

Axel likes to visit Granny. She often arranges treats for her little guest.

"Today we are eating blueberries," Granny says and pours the berries into two bowls.

4

The doorbell rings and Granny goes to open it. Becca from next door has come to return a book she borrowed.

Axel looks impatiently at his bowl of blueberries. *I hope Becca leaves soon*, he thinks. *I cannot wait any longer!*

G ranny and Becca's conversation goes on and on in the hallway.

"I think I can taste these berries, just a little bit," Axel decides.

He carefully picks up the bowl, but it falls to the floor.

7

Dark berries roll all over the kitchen floor. There is a heap of them on Granny's light-colored rug, too!

"What a mess! I have to pick up everything before Granny returns!"

Axel carefully picks up all the berries from under the table and behind the chair legs.

"Now I'll pick up the berries on the rug. Then everything will be fine!"

A sad surprise awaits Axel. Each blueberry has left a splash of color on the pale rug.

"I'll wash the rug while Granny takes a nap in the afternoon," Axel decides.

11

Axel quickly flips the rug over. On the other side, it looks clean.

"Let's have our treat now," Granny says cheerfully as she returns to the kitchen.

Axel slowly eats a few blueberries.

But the blueberries don't taste as delicious as usual. The little boy is worried about the stains on the rug.

"Are you tired, my dear? Is it a good time for a nap?" Granny asks.

Axel nods.

15

Soon Granny is snoring on the couch, and Axel lies in a beanbag chair. He is not sleeping.

Now it's time to wash the rug, he thinks. *I'll do it in the bathtub. I know where Granny stores detergent.*

The rug is heavy, but Axel finally gets it into the tub.

Now I need some warm water and detergent, Alex thinks. *Soon the rug will be cleaner than ever!*

Axel hopes Granny will be pleased.

There are many kinds of jars and packages on the shelves of Granny's cleaning closet.

"Hard to choose!" Axel sighs.

He can't read yet. So he decides to put different kinds of soap in the water.

Alex lets the rug soak. But when he checks it, he sees a big problem.

"Oh no! The color of the rug is changing!" Axel is worried.

He has to wake up Granny and tell her what happened.

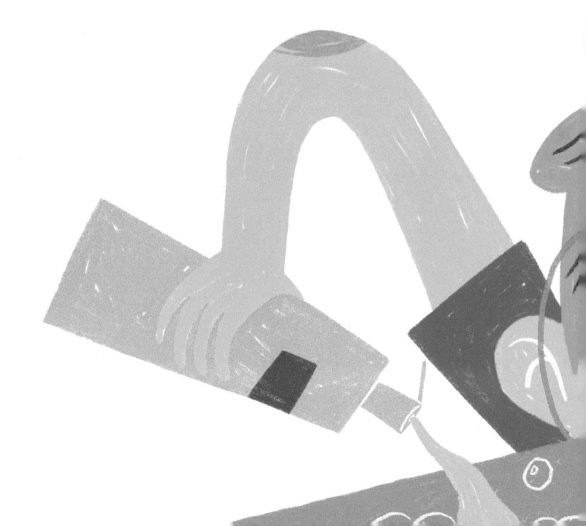

Sleepy Granny comes to the bathroom to investigate the situation.

"Oh, you used detergent—and bleach," Granny says anxiously. "You didn't splash any bleach on yourself, did you?"

Axel shakes his head. "The bleach only went in the tub."

Grandma looks relieved. "Good. Bleach can be harmful to your skin."

Granny rinses the rug thoroughly. Now it looks quite interesting with white spots dotting its colorful background.

"Pretty artistic! Maybe we'll use the rug as a wall decoration when it's dry," Granny says.

Axel is relieved that Granny isn't angry.

"Please forgive me, Granny," Axel says.

"Of course," Granny says gently. "Every-thing turned out fine!"

They agree to wash the rug together next time—and Granny will choose the right soap!

CPSIA information can be obtained
at www.ICGtesting.com
Printed in the USA
BVHW020927190821
614775BV00006B/219

9 789523 574687